Dancing on the Moon

Dancing On The Moon

Published by Gatekeeper Press
2167 Stringtown Rd, Suite 109
Columbus, OH 43123-2989
www.GatekeeperPress.com

Library of Congress Control Number: 2021950469

ISBN (hardcover): 9781662921926
ISBN (paperback): 9781662921933
eISBN: 9781662921940

Dancing on the Moon

Mina London

Maliyah London

Illustration by Ananta Mohanta

gatekeeper press

Columbus, Ohio

Hi! I am Nala.
When I grow up,
I want to dance on the moon.

Did you know
that we can be anything we want to be
when we get older?

Yup, like an astronaut or even a ballerina!

My mommy always tells me
if I can dream it, then I can achieve it.
She says to find my joy and
share it with the world.

I love dancing under the moonlight.
ONE DAY...
I'm going to shine bright on that big,
beautiful moon.

At school, we shared our hopes and dreams with the class, and everyone laughed at me.

They said there is no way that I can dance on the moon... and that made me feel blue and full of gloom. I started to doubt myself.

Then, suddenly– I remembered
what my mommy taught me.

My light is magical!
I am one-of-a-kind,
so I should always be truly me.
No matter what anyone thinks of me,
I can be anything that I dream to be.

We're born to stand out.
When something simply "fits in" it is
too easy to be completely unnoticed.

When something stands
out you cannot help noticing.
You cannot help but have
your attention drawn to it.

So, you see, I don't care in any way what someone else may think or say about me.

I am not confined to the limitations of what they believe is possible for me because my mommy taught me that I can be anything!

I will not dim my light!
Like the moon,
I am here to shine bright.

Printed in the USA
CPSIA information can be obtained
at www.ICGtesting.com
LVHW080846011023
759462LV00021B/25